The Woman Fooled the Fairies

Written by Rose Impey

Illustrated by Nick Schon

Collins

Chapter 1

There was once a woman who baked the best cakes
in the whole wide world.

Her scones were scrumptious.
Her tarts were terrific.
Her biscuits were brilliant.
But her cakes ... oh, her cakes took your breath away.
People came from miles around to buy them.

3

The fairies loved the woman's cakes too.
But they didn't want to *buy* them. Day after day,
they waited under the woman's window.

They hoped she would leave a cake out to cool.
But the woman was far too wise for that.

4

So the fairies said to themselves,
"If we can't steal a cake,
we'll steal the cake-maker!"

Chapter 2

One warm summer's night, the woman was walking home through the woods.

First she heard a hundred little whispers.
Then she felt a flurry of fairy wings around her face.

Soon she felt too tired to take another step.
She just had to lie down and close her eyes.

When she opened her eyes she found herself inside
the fairies' palace.

"Whatever do you want with me?" she asked
the fairies.
"Bake us a cake," they demanded.
"Now! We won't take you home till you do."

8

The woman sighed and took her apron out of her bag.
"Show me the kitchen," she said.
So the fairies led her there, dancing and singing as they went.

The woman looked around her. The fairies hadn't a thing she
needed. That was lucky.
"Oh dear, oh dear," she sighed. "Where is the flour?"
The fairies looked puzzled. They had no flour.
"I have plenty of flour," said the woman, "in my cottage."
The fairies flew straight to the woman's cottage.

In no time they were back, with a huge bag of flour.
"*Now* will you make us a cake?" they panted.
"I will, I will," said the woman. "But where is the sugar?"
The fairies looked surprised. They had no sugar.
"And butter," the woman laughed. "I have both in
my kitchen."

The fairies flew so fast they almost met themselves
coming back.
"*Now* will you make us a cake?" they said, even louder
this time.

"I will, I will," said the woman. "But I must have eggs."
The fairies looked furious. They had no eggs.
"There's a dozen in my pantry," the woman told them.

In less than a minute the fairies were back, juggling the eggs in the air.

"*Now* will you make us a cake?" they cried, louder
than ever.

"I will, I will," said the woman, "when I have a big
enough bowl."

"A bowl?" they squealed at the tops of their tiny voices.

"There's one on my kitchen dresser," said the woman.

"And bring my wooden spoon," she called after them.

14

It took ten fairies to carry the woman's mixing bowl.
And another three to carry the spoon.

"NOW WILL YOU MAKE US A CAKE?" they almost
screamed at her. Fairies have very short tempers.
"Oh I will, I will," said the woman. "Now that I have
everything I need."

Chapter 3

First the woman beat the butter and the sugar together.
Then she stirred in the eggs and the flour.

The fairies watched her, their little heads turning in time with
the spoon.

When it was mixed, the woman shook her head again.
"How can I bake a cake with no baking tin?"
"Where is it, where is it?" squealed the fairies, half way out of the door.
"In the cupboard under the sink ..."

The fairies soon came back, beating on the tin as if it were a drum. It was enough to give the woman a headache.

She emptied the mixture into the baking tin.
Then she looked around her again.

"Where can I bake it?" demanded the woman.
"My tin is far too big to fit in your tiny oven."
The fairies looked as if they might burst into tears.
"Of course," said the woman, "I have a nice big oven at
home ..."

Before she had finished speaking,
she found herself being carried through the air.

The fairies were tired of the woman by now.
They tossed her between them like a pancake.

But she landed safely in her own kitchen, where she stood grinning at them.

Then the fairies knew they had been tricked. They looked so sad, the woman almost felt sorry for them. She said she would still bake their cake.

But the fairies were too tired to care. They flew home to their beds.

20

The next morning, when the cake was cool,
the woman took it to the fairies' palace.

She left the cake where she knew they would find it.
It seemed a shame to wake them up, when they had had
such a busy night!

A Story Map

Ideas for reading

Written by Linda Pagett B.Ed (hons), M.Ed
Lecturer and Educational Consultant

Reading objectives:
- become increasingly familiar with and retelling a wider range of fairy stories
- predict what might happen on the basis of what has been read so far
- discuss and clarify the meanings of words
- make inferences on the basis of what is being said and done
- explain and discuss their understanding of books

Spoken language objectives:
- use spoken language to develop understanding through speculating, imagining and exploring ideas
- use relevant strategies to build their vocabulary
- maintain attention and participate actively in collaborative conversations
- give well-structured descriptions, explanations and narratives for different purposes, including for expressing feelings
- participate in discussions and role play

Curriculum links: PSHE

Interest words: scrumptious, fairies, furious, pantry, emptied

Word count: 796

Build a context for reading

This text can be read over two reading sessions.
- Introduce the book to the children, and discuss the cover and blurb. Ask children to skim through the pages up to p21, looking at the pictures.
- Discuss what sort of story this is and what the children think is going to happen.
- Draw children's attention to unfamiliar words and discuss decoding strategies, for example, scrumptious and pantry begin with 'easy' words scrum and pan.
- Explore the background detail in the illustrations, and ask children what they can tell about the characters in the story from these details, e.g pp2–3 shows the woman loves making cakes.

Understand and apply reading strategies

- Remind children of their strategies for unknown words (e.g. *furious, pantry*), including making 'good guesses', where they can explain their choice of word.
- Ask the children to read the story independently and silently up to p21.
- As they read, ask children to think about key questions: *Is the woman frightened of the fairies? Why did she keep making them go back to her cottage? Were the fairies angry? Who gets their own way in the end?*